this VeggieTales® gift book belongs to:

_____

_____
from

_____
date

Published by Howard Publishing Co., Inc.
3117 North 7th Street, West Monroe, Louisiana 71291-2227
www.howardpublishing.com

05   06   07   08   09   10   11   12   13   14   10   9   8   7   6   5   4   3   2   1

Photography by Chrys Howard and LinDee Loveland © 2005 Howard Publishing Co., Inc.

ISBN 1-58229-451-8 (I Can Be Your Friend)

I Can Be Your Friend. Music and lyrics by Phil Vischer.
© 1995 Bob & Larry Publishing (ASCAP)

I Can Be Your Friend!

written by Phil Vischer
illustrated by Casey Jones and Karen Poth

Whether we're young or old, skinny or stout, this classic VeggieTales® song reminds us that "the inside is the part that we're supposed to care about".

God makes each one of us different. And those differences are what makes us all special in his eyes.

Sing along with the enclosed CD as you read the words and enjoy the pictures that bring this special song to life!

A *girl* with BRACES on her teeth or FRECKLES on her nose?

in all COLORS, shapes, and sizes.

He **LOVES** them **very** much,

and
what we **need** to realize is...

Instead, we need to look on them in **LOVE** and sing this song:

I can be your friend.
I can be your
FRIEND.
Any day,
in any weather,
we can be
friends and play
TOGETHER!

But the iNSiDE is the part that we're supposed to care about.

I can be your
FRIEND.
I can be your friend.
If your hair is
RED or yellow,
we can have lunch.
I'll share my
jello!

REMEMBER! God made you special, and he loves you very much!

Collect the entire gift book series!
Perfect for any occasion!

There's nothing scarier to children than thinking they're in the dark, facing all kinds of monsters, with no one to protect them. *God Is Bigger!* is a fun way to remind children that God is always near and strong enough to take care of them.

Based on the best-loved Silly Song with Larry, *Oh, Where Is My Hairbrush?* is sure to delight every VeggieTales® fan. Bright, colorful illustrations, as well as a sing-along CD of "The Hairbrush Song," will make this book a keepsake that your children will always treasure.

Do you ever wonder why we tell everyone about our day except for the One who is powerful and loving enough to help us through the next one? *My Day*, with its colorful pictures and fun messages, shows children how to develop a relationship with God through prayer.

CD of accompanying VeggieTales© song included with each book!